P9-CCH-242

# SUGAR CREEK GANG
# THE
# KILLER BEAR

# SUGAR CREEK GANG

# THE
# KILLER BEAR

Original title:
**We Killed a Bear**

**Paul Hutchens**

**MOODY PRESS • CHICAGO**

Copyright 1940 by
Wm. B. Eerdmans Publishing Company

Copyright Renewal 1968 by
Paul Hutchens

MOODY PRESS EDITION 1970

All rights in this book are reserved. No part may be
reproduced in any manner without permission in writing from the author except brief quotations used in
connection with a review in a magazine or newspaper.

ISBN 0-8024-4802-X

35 37 39 40 38 36

*Printed in the United States of America*

*To*
*my five brothers,*
*Leo, Forest, Haven, Lester and Carl*
*the best pals a boy ever had,*
*and who lived and played*
*with me along and in*
*the real*
*SUGAR CREEK*

# 1

I<small>T WAS</small> D<small>RAGONFLY</small> who first saw the bear—
a big hairy, black thing that looked more like
one of my dad's big hogs than anything else.

None of us boys had ever seen an honest-to-
goodness wild bear, although we'd all been to
the zoo and the circus and had watched bears
juggling rope balls and doing different kinds of
acrobatic stunts. Naturally we had read a lot
of bear stories, having borrowed the books from
our school and public libraries, but we had never dreamed that a bear story would happen to
us, the kind of story that would make any boy's
hair stand right up on end.

Perhaps I'd better explain right away that
when I say "us" I mean The Sugar Creek Gang,
which is the name of our gang of six boys. We

have crazy names like nearly all boys do—that is, all of us except me. I am just plain Bill, which is short for William, which name I don't like. My middle name is Jasper. I don't like that either.

Dragonfly's real name is Roy Gilbert, but we call him Dragonfly because he is always seeing important things first, and his eyes grow big when he does, making him look kind of like a dragonfly, or a walleyed pike or something.

Then there is Big Jim, the leader of our gang who has been a Boy Scout; and Little Jim, the grandest little fellow you ever saw and as good as a million dollars worth of gold. Little Jim is my very best friend, except for Poetry. Poetry is the name we've given to Leslie Thompson because he knows maybe a hundred poems by heart and is always quoting one of them, much to Circus' disgust. Circus is our acrobat and can juggle baseballs better than any trained bear, and is always climbing trees and acting like a monkey and looking like one, and is almost as mischievous as Poetry, although I don't think anybody else could be that mischievous. Poetry is very fat, almost as big around as a barrel.

That's all of us: Big Jim, our leader; Little Jim, the best Christian any boy ever saw; Poetry, whose voice is squawky like a duck with a bad cold; Dragonfly, whose eyes are as keen as an Indian's; and Circus, whose Dad is always getting drunk and giving him a licking whether he needs it or not. Circus has four sisters, one of them is only about a month old, just one day younger than my own little sister, Charlotte Ann, who really ought to belong to our gang too, 'cause she's so grand. But she can't because she's too little and especially because she's a girl, and girls can't belong to a gang of boys. No boy would stand for that.

Let me see—oh, yes! I ought to tell you that Poetry has a tent in his back yard where our gang sometimes has our meetings, when we don't have them at the springs or the big syca-more tree, or up on the top of the hill on the east side of the woods, where there are a big rock and a big patch of wild strawberries.

Well, I'd better get busy telling you about the bear. When we first saw him—her, rath-er—she was away down along Sugar Creek right out in the middle of the swamp, wallowing in the mud, like black bears do in the summertime when it's terribly hot. That's why I told you the bear looked like one of my dad's big black hogs.

Dragonfly had come over to my house right after dinner that day. And because it was so terribly hot, my dad and mom decided we could go swimming—only we had to wait an hour first because it's dangerous to go in swimming right after a meal. You might get cramps or something, which is kind of like "local paralysis," and you can't move your legs and you might drown. You know, maybe I'm going to be a doctor some day. That's how I happen to know the medical names for some of these things.

It seemed like it was ten times hotter than it had been the day when Dragonfly and I caught a big black bass.

"Whew!" I said when I'd finished dinner. "It's *terribly* hot!" Then I said, "May I be excused, please?" That is what you're supposed to say when you leave the table before the others do.

"Certainly," Dad said.

But Mom said, "I'm sorry, Billy, but I'll have

to have help with the dishes today. It's wash day, you know."

I looked at all those dirty dishes on the table —the plates and cups and saucers and my big blue and white mug out of which I drank milk three times a day. And when I saw all the silverware—forks and knives and spoons—and a great big stack of other dishes, it actually hurt 'way down inside of me, 'cause I'd a whole lot rather be dunking myself in the old swimming hole in Sugar Creek than sloshing soapy water over dirty dishes—*hot* water at that! On a terribly hot day! I couldn't help but wish Charlotte Ann would hurry up and grow big enough so she could help Mom. Whatever makes baby girls grow so slowly anyway?

Then I happened to think how much my mom loved me and how hard she had to work all the time to keep my dad's clothes clean—and the house—and get the meals and take care of Charlotte Ann, and how very tired she looked. So I just made myself smile and say cheerfully, "Sure! I'll help you! I can't go swimming for an hour anyway!"

But there was another reason why I wanted

11

to help Mom, which I can't take time to tell you now. But when I was in the other room looking at Charlotte Ann and watching her drink her milk out of a bottle, I heard Dad say to Mom, "There's a little secret I want to tell you about Bill when I get a chance. You know —"

Then he told her something I'd told him that very morning—a secret that was the most important secret of my whole life. But I think I'll let you guess what it was.

Pretty soon the dishes were finished and Dragonfly was there, and in a jiffy he and I, both barefoot and with our overalls rolled up so our toes wouldn't get caught in the cuffs and send us sprawling head over heels, went scuttling like wild things across the road, over the old rail fence and through the woods to the spring where we knew the gang would be waiting for us.

In about ten or fifteen minutes we all were there—all except Little Jim who took piano lessons and had to practice a whole hour every day, a half hour in the morning and a half hour right after dinner. He had taken lessons last summer too and could play a lot of things. Some day, maybe, he'd be a famous concert pianist. That little fellow knew the names of nearly all the famous musicians, such as Bach and Beethoven and Wagner and Liszt and Damrosch and a lot of others. He even knew stories about different ones. Little Jim's mother was a wonderful musician and she played the piano in our church on Sundays.

Did you ever hear a flock of blackbirds in the autumn, getting ready to fly south for the winter? Their voices are all raspy from chirping so much, and they seem to be squawking to the leaves of the trees to look out, 'cause pretty soon Jack Frost'll get 'em and they'll all have to die and be buried in a white grave.

Well, when our gang gets together after we've been separated for a while we're almost as noisy as a hundred blackbirds. Blackbirds are what the winged notes on Little Jim's music sheets look like. They almost make a fellow dizzy to even think of trying to play them.

Pretty soon Little Jim was there, carrying his stick which he had cut from an ash limb. He nearly always carried a stick. He came running down the hill with his straw hat in one hand and his stick in the other, his short little legs pumping like a boy in a bicycle race, and with the dark curls on his head shining in the sun.

In a few jiffies we were all running as fast as we could toward the swimming hole.

"Last one in's a bear's tail," Circus cried over his shoulder. He was the fastest runner of all of us. He had his shirt off even before he got there, taking it off on the run. He was the first one in, all right, and I was the last. I was a little slow on purpose 'cause I didn't want Little Jim to be the bear's tail.

"Bear's don't have tails," Poetry yelled to Circus.

"Neither do cows jump over moons," Circus yelled back.

That started Poetry off:

> Hey, diddle, diddle, the cat and the fiddle,
> The cow jumped over the moon.

Circus made a dive for Poetry, caught him around the neck, ducked him a couple of times and said, quoting a poem himself:

This is the cow with the crumpled horn,
   That tossed the dog, that worried the cat,
   That caught the rat, that ate the malt
      That lay in the house that Jack built.

Poetry looked disgusted at being called a cow, not being able to help it because he was so fat.

Well, we had water fights, and diving and swimming contests until we were all cooled off. Then we dressed and started looking for different kinds of shells. All of us boys were collecting shells for a hobby that summer.

I don't know how we got to talking about bears, but we did. And I'll have to admit I felt kind of creepy when Dragonfly told us a true story about how a real bear caught and buried a man alive once. We were down along the edge of the swamp, lying in the grass, right close to the big hollow sycamore tree, resting and thinking about how we'd caught the bank robber here just one month ago.

"It happened away out west along the Colorado river," Dragonfly said. "First the bear—it was a great big grizzly bear—caught and buried a colt. Grizzly bears cache their food, you know, like dogs do a bone or something, then they come back later and dig it up and eat it. Well, when the owner of the colt found out where it was buried and tried to shoot the bear, old Grizzly just rushed at him and knocked him down. The man's gun barrel struck against his own head and knocked him unconscious. Then old Grizzly, thinking the man was dead, picked him up and buried him right beside the colt. Then it dug up the colt, ate some of it for his dinner and went away. Of course, the man wasn't buried very deep and he could still breathe. Pretty soon he came to and dug his way out and hurried away before the bear decided it was time for supper.

"That's a true story," Dragonfly said as he finished.

"But there aren't any bears around here, so we don't need to be afraid," Big Jim said, looking at Little Jim, who was holding onto his stick with both hands as if he were beginning to be scared.

"Not any grizzly bears," I said, " 'cause they don't live in this part of America," I'd been reading about bears in a book in my dad's library. My dad had the most interesting books for a boy to read.

Pretty soon we began to feel hot again, so we decided to follow the old footpath that leads through the swamp. It was nearly always cool there because there were little springs that came out of the hillside and oozed their way along through the mud, making it cool even on the hottest days.

We were still thinking about bears, anyway I was, and Little Jim was holding onto his stick very tight, when suddenly Dragonfly said, "Phsst!"

# 2

WE ALL STOPPED DEAD in our tracks and Little Jim's face turned white. I guess he was still thinking about the man that had been buried by a bear, because he had been walking close to Big Jim and holding his stick tighter than anything.

Dragonfly was down on his hands and knees peering through the foliage of a swamp rosebush. Just then we heard a crashing and a snapping of underbrush like something about as big as an elephant was running away, and I could feel a prickly sensation under my straw hat as if my red hair was trying to stand up on end and couldn't because of my hat being on too tight.

19

Of course I knew that bears hardly ever attacked anybody unless they were very hungry. This one *might* be hungry, I thought. I got my binoculars up to my eyes real quick but couldn't see anything but a lot of trees and briars and sedge and little ponds of water.

Suddenly I gasped out loud! I'd *seen* it! It was black and hairy and all covered with mud and it was breaking its way through the swamp like it was almost as scared as Little Jim—or maybe Bill Collins.

Knowing bears don't generally attack people, and being able to *feel* it, are two different things. I was actually shaking all over, and for a minute we were all so scared we couldn't talk. I looked around quick to see if we were all there and all right, and we were. But Circus was already halfway up an elm sapling, not because he was afraid but because he wanted to see where the bear or whatever it was, was going.

Pretty soon we all found our voices again but we didn't sound like a lot of scolding blackbirds and we didn't look like the notes on Little Jim's music, although I couldn't help but wish we had wings. We sounded more like ghosts whispering to each other in a haunted house in low frightened voices. That is, all except Dragonfly. He had a grin on his face about the size of a jack-o'-lantern and he looked as if he knew something important.

"Aw!" he said loftily. "What are you so scared for? It wasn't anything but somebody's old hog wallowing in the mud. Come on, I'll show you!"

Well, I'd seen something black and hairy and muddy running through the undergrowth and it *had* looked like one of my dad's big black hogs. Yet, I remembered that black bears hunt out swampy places in the hot weather, and I still believed it might have been a bear. I could see, however, that it wouldn't do to say so, or they'd make fun of me, and I didn't want to frighten Little Jim again.

I reached up and picked a green cluster of winged seeds from the ash tree and started chewing one of them. Then I broke off two or three yellow-green leaves which were about nine inches long, each one having seven or nine leaflets and, taking off my hat, I tucked them up

21

inside the crown so my head would keep cool when we got out in the sun again.

Big Jim looked at his watch and, because it was four o'clock, we decided maybe we'd better go swimming again before we went home. That was another one of Big Jim's rules: we all had to help our folks with the chores, and we had to do it cheerfully. Besides, we had to get them done good and early all this week and next because the churches in town and our church, which was out in the country in a beautiful shady grove, were having what is called a Good News Crusade, and most of us boys went every night.

Little Jim's mother, being the best pianist in the whole country, played the piano at the meetings. There was a big brown tent pitched right in the park in our town, with long board benches with comfortable backs. There was a big platform for the choir, a grand piano and everything. But I'll tell you more about that a little later 'cause something very important happened there.

On the way to the swimming hole, Poetry and I walked together. He had a mysterious

look on his face and he began to quote a verse
from "Christmas Secrets," which goes:

> The air is full of mystery
> And secrets are a-wing;
> And if you happen on one,
> Don't tell a single thing.

The rest of the gang had gone on ahead. Because Poetry and I liked each other a lot, we
walked close together with our arms around
each other—that is, his arm was around me, and
mine was as far around him as I could reach.

"Do you think it was a hog?" he asked, his
squawky voice more squawky than usual.

"I don't know," I said, beginning to feel my
spine tingling again.

"I think it was a bear," Poetry said. The way
he said it made me stop and look at him.

"It was somebody's black hog," I said, half
hoping it wasn't. I even turned around quick
to see if maybe there was a bear behind us, but
there wasn't.

Just then Poetry shoved his hand deep into
his overall pocket and pulled out a dirty bit of
something that looked half like hair and half

23

like fur. "Bears shed in the summer, don't they?" he asked. He had that mysterious, detectivelike look on his face.

"Where'd you get that?" I asked.

"I picked it up back there in the mud—and here's some more. I found this caught on a rose-bush."

Well, it looked like the real thing, all right, but we didn't say anything about it to the rest of the gang.

I got home in plenty of time to help Dad with the chores. After I'd gathered the eggs he sent me down the lane to the pasture for the cows.

"Don't forget to shut the gate," he said. And then he said something that almost made me jump out of my shoes—that is, if I hadn't been barefoot. He said, "Several of our pigs are miss-ing and it looks like somebody's been a little careless about shutting gates."

"*What!*" I said, staring at him, and remem-bering suddenly that the book I'd read had said that bears like pork better than anything else, and that they sometimes raided the farm or barnyard and stole little pigs.

24

Dad looked back at me kind of hard for saying "What" so foolishly. I guess he must have thought I was trying to deny the fact that I sometimes forgot to shut the gate. He started to say something, then changed his mind and walked away. I hurried down the lane after the cows, thinking all the way and saying to myself, "Bears like pork. Bears are crazy about pork. Bears steal little pigs."

Believe me, I shut the gate good and tight when I left it. I wanted in the worst way to tell Dad what I'd seen down in the old swamp, but I didn't dare to because Poetry had made me promise I wouldn't.

My next chore was feeding the horses so I climbed up in the haymow of our barn and, with my favorite pitchfork, began to throw down big bunches of sweet-smelling alfalfa hay.

For a month I'd been having a strange feeling every time I was in our haymow, because away up in a corner, tucked in a crack in a log, was my little black leather New Testament. You know I think every boy's parents ought to buy a neat little New Testament for him, not a cheap one but an honest-to-goodness leather-bound one that a boy can be proud of and that won't wear out so quick—that is, if he reads it every day like he's supposed to. Even poor parents can afford to, if they really want to and save their money a little at a time.

You see, Little Jim wasn't the only Christian in the Sugar Creek Gang. Poetry had been one a long time, and Big Jim, too; and I'd been one just about a month. In fact, just two days after Charlotte Ann was born, I was "born again," which is an expression the Bible uses for becoming a Christian. It's a wonderful thing, the most important thing in the world, in fact, 'cause if you aren't born again, you'll never go to heaven when you die.

The reason I'd left my New Testament in the crack in the log was to sort of remind God that I was praying for Circus' dad that he'd be born again so he wouldn't get drunk anymore and so Circus' family would go to church on Sundays like all families are supposed to.

I'd made up my mind to leave my little New Testament there until Circus' dad became a Christian. Every day I climbed up there and read it and talked to Jesus, which is the same as praying. Maybe some boys would be afraid to do that, but why should they when Jesus is the best Friend a boy ever had, and came all the way down here from heaven to save us and was a Boy Himself once!

Well, when I'd thrown down all the hay I was supposed to, I climbed away up into the corner again. And because my dad might wonder why I was staying so long, I didn't take time to read. I just dropped down on my knees, shut my eyes and told Jesus several important things, kind of like a boy telling his best friend something. I don't know what I said, but I knew I felt very sorry for Circus for not having Christian parents and because his dad spent so much money for beer and whiskey that the children didn't have enough to eat and couldn't buy decent clothes so they could go to Sunday school and church.

Circus' dad had been in the hospital too, and still didn't feel very well, although he was able to work some.

*"Bill!"* my dad called up the ladder.

"Coming!" I said, and hurried back down and fed the horses.

# 3

THERE MUST HAVE BEEN a hundred boys in the big brown tent that night, and hundreds and hundreds of grownup people—and a lot of girls too. All our gang was there, except Dragonfly whose folks didn't go to church much.

We all managed to sit together in the same row, although Mom and Dad had made it plain to me before we left home that I couldn't sit next to Poetry. You see, they couldn't trust us together 'cause he was so mischievous and we might get to laughing or something.

I wish every boy in the world could have had parents like mine and Little Jim's. Little Jim's mom had on a pretty blue dress and a neat little blue and silver hat perched on top of her brown

29

hair, reminding me of a bird or something, and her fingers just flew over the piano keys, up and down and across and everything, making me like the gospel songs better than ever and making everybody want to sing.

Once I stopped singing and looked at Little Jim, who was sitting beside me. His big blue eyes were shining with pride and I could see he thought his mother was better even than an angel.

Right across the aisle and about three rows back, sat my mom and dad and little Charlotte Ann, my baby sister. Dad saw me looking at them and his big, bushy, blackish-red eyebrows were straight, so I knew he liked me all right and that I wasn't doing anything I shouldn't. I could see Mom's hair with the silver streaks in it, showing just beneath her hat. I liked Mom's hat 'cause it had pretty embroidered flowers on the front of it and she had such a pleasant face. I guess maybe I'd seen her face a million times and I never got tired of looking at it. When little Charlotte Ann was born, Mom's face looked happier than I'd ever seen it in my whole life.

Charlotte Ann didn't cry much anymore, although she nearly always managed to cry a little in church, like most babies do, even when they're good all the rest of the time.

There was a band with clarinets and trombones and violins and cellos and cornets. The song leader, who wore a brown coat with white trousers, played a cornet himself. Once I looked at Circus, who was sitting on the other side of Little Jim and between Poetry and me, and he was watching that shining cornet, kind of like a hungry boy looking in at a big display window full of good things to eat, and knowing he couldn't have any. And I thought—well, I thought about my little New Testament back home, away up in our dark haymow, and I wondered if Someone up in heaven was looking down at it and remembering my prayer and maybe getting ready to answer it tonight. I knew that Circus' dad was standing outside the tent somewhere listening.

There was a row of ministers sitting on the platform just behind the pulpit, and I couldn't help but think how kind they looked. It seemed wonderful that those great big strong men loved

31

the Saviour and had given their whole lives to tell people about Him, even if I was a little bit afraid of some ministers because of their having such big voices and being so important.

A little later one of the ministers stood up to pray. He had such a deep voice and used such long words that it made God seem very far away, and his voice had a little growl in it, like a bear's voice.

Just then I thought of Poetry and looked at him, and would you believe it? His mischievous blue eyes looked right straight into mine; and before I could stop myself, I'd snickered out loud. Just that very second I thought of my dad too and I looked back at him, and he was looking straight at me with his long blackish-red eyebrows down and with a scowl on his forehead.

Well, I was sorry, but I knew that wouldn't help 'cause I'd promised to be good in church and not get into mischief.

But let me tell you about the important thing that happened that night. The meeting kept right on going, band and choir music, solos and quartets and a very interesting sermon.

You know, when I'd first started praying for Circus' dad, I'd sort of expected God to answer my prayer right away, anyway in a week or two. I didn't realize then that a person had to hear the gospel preached first, and that nobody ever gets saved unless somebody tells him about Jesus. Besides, God won't just come to a man's heart and batter it open in order to get in. You have to open that door yourself. So I'd decided if I had to wait a long time I would, but I would keep right on praying.

Anyway, the minister who preached that night, talked about the "Home." I knew Circus' dad was outside somewhere listening, but I certainly didn't expect him to be much interested. That's why I was so surprised when I got my prayer answered.

This is the way it happened. Every now and then during the sermon I glanced over at Circus to see how he liked it. But I didn't need to worry about him not liking it. He was listening for all he was worth. Good old Circus, I thought, with his monkey face, his strong athletic body, and his pretty brown hair combed nice and straight. He'd shined his shabby old shoes the best he could and his mom had pressed his almost threadbare suit and made it look all right. He'd even cleaned his finger nails and washed his neck and ears, which I knew he didn't like to do. There he was, sitting up straight and listening with shining eyes, in spite of knowing that as soon as the meeting was over he'd have to go home to a weathered old house with poor furniture and worn-out rugs on the floor and a swearing, drinking father who didn't like him.

I remembered the time about a month ago when Circus' dad had been drunk on the same night they had a new baby at their house, and Circus had stayed all night at my house. He and I were upstairs undressing, and he got tears in his eyes and doubled up his fists and looked terribly fierce 'cause he was so mad at the people that made and sold beer and whiskey. That was the night he had said, with his voice all trembly, "I wish they'd just *once* take a picture of my dad when he's drunk and looking like he did uptown tonight and put *that* in their old newspapers and magazines! I bet *that* wouldn't make anybody want to buy any!"

Well, pretty soon the sermon was over and

the minister announced that there was going to be a short prayer meeting in a curtained-off corner of the tent, beginning right away. He said he'd like all the Sunday school teachers and superintendents to stay, and to come forward and go into the little room while everybody was singing the last song, which was Big Jim's favorite:

> Just as I am without one plea,
> But that Thy blood was shed for me.

Then the minister said in his big kind voice, "No doubt there are many here tonight who have felt the Spirit drawing you toward God. You realize that you, like all the rest of us, need Christ as your Saviour. Will you come forward too and let us explain to you from the Bible exactly how to be saved? And if there are any of your friends who wish to come with you, they may feel free to do so."

Maybe those aren't the exact words he used, but it was something like that. I thought it was a nice way to say it, and I just knew somebody would go. A person couldn't hear a sermon like that and not want to.

Everybody was standing and singing. And because my dad was a Sunday school teacher, he handed Charlotte Ann over to Mom and started down the grassy aisle toward the little curtained-off corner of the tent, carrying his Bible with him, which he always took to church anyway.

Pretty soon people were going forward from all around us, while Little Jim's mom played and the choir and everybody was singing, even the people in the band, 'cause the band never played during what they called the "invitation hymn."

Between verses the minister said different things, urging people *not* to come because he was asking them to, but to obey God's voice. They could tell whether God was speaking to them if they felt something tugging at their heartstrings, he said.

I looked down at Little Jim and he was standing there with tears in his eyes, with his hands gripping the back of the seat in front of him. And all the time people were going forward from all over the tent. So I leaned over to little Jim and said, "What's the matter?"

Little Jim gulped and his voice choked and he whispered, "C-Circus. I—I want him to be saved tonight."

And do you know, I couldn't stand to see Little Jim's tears. It was kind of like our old iron pitcher pump back home when it runs down. You have to pour water in the top; and then if you pump real hard for a minute, the water'll come and you can pump gallons and gallons. It's called "priming." Well, Little Jim's tears primed mine, and before I knew it a tear had tumbled out of one of my eyes and splashed right down on the songbook I was holding.

I gulped and started singing as hard as I could, looking straight ahead of me. And while I looked, it just seemed like the minister and the choir and the tent faded away and I could see a little leather book tucked away in a crack in a log up in the corner of our haymow.

Just that minute there was a rustling beside me and I knew that somebody from our row was trying to get out into the aisle. I looked quick to see who it was, and it was Circus. In a jiffy he was gone, and all that I could see of him was his square shoulders and the top of his pretty brown head as he hurried down the aisle toward the little room kind of like a soldier marching in a parade.

The minister saw him coming and stepped down off the platform to meet him and to shake hands with him before he let him go into the little room. Then the minister's kind voice said to all of us, "I think I'd rather see a fine boy like this come to Christ than anybody else in the whole world."

Then it happened. It happened so quick I could hardly believe my eyes. Somebody was hurrying down the aisle right past us—running in fact, and crying and saying, "That's my boy! That's my boy! I want to be saved too!" And it was Circus' dad. He threw his arms around Circus and they went into the little room together.

I was glad my dad was already in there, 'cause I knew that he knew the Bible well enough to show Circus' dad how to be saved, although the ministers that had been on the platform were all in there too.

Pretty soon there was another rustling beside

me, and in a jiffy Little Jim was gone. He scuttled down that aisle kind of like a little chipmunk running toward a stump along Sugar Creek.

Well, I knew Little Jim was already saved, and I knew he'd gone in just to be with Circus, 'cause he liked him so well. So before I knew it, I was gone too, down the beautiful green aisle, past the minister and Little Jim's mother at the piano and into the little tent room.

There were maybe thirty or forty people there, all kneeling; and over in a corner, kneeling by a bench, was my big dad with his arms around Circus' dad who was still crying; and beside them was Circus and Little Jim, and Little Jim's arm was around Circus and—well, it was the prettiest sight I ever saw, prettier even than a sunset with red and gold and purple clouds; prettier than the maple and ash and oak trees along Sugar Creek in autumn.

In a jiffy I was down beside Little Jim. And before the prayer meeting was over, all the Sugar Creek gang was there except Dragonfly, kneeling all in a row. And I got to thinking while I was there that if all the boys in the world could do what we were doing right that minute, when they grew up, there wouldn't be any gangsters or thieves or drunkards or broken-hearted mothers.

It was great! Right that minute I decided something, and that was that when I grew up and became a doctor, I wasn't only going to be a good doctor; but I was going to be a *saved* doctor who knew how to lead other people to Jesus like my dad did.

When the meeting was over and we had gone home and the car was in the garage, I asked my dad for his flashlight.

"What for?" he said.

"Oh—'cause! I want to go outdoors awhile."

He looked at me, started to say no, then changed his mind.

So, with the flashlight in my hand, I went out and across the barnyard to our barn door, opened it and went inside. There was old Mixy, our black and white cat, mewing on a log, and I could hear the crunch, crunch of our horses' teeth as they ate their hay. Then I climbed the wooden ladder up into our haymow. I didn't stay up there very long, not more than a jiffy, but when I came down again, I had my little New Testament in my hip pocket.

At the foot of the ladder I scooped Mixy up in my arms and hugged her and said, "Mixy, you're the nicest, prettiest cat in all the world! All the whole wide world!" I carried her in my arms all the way across the barnyard to the house, then I let her down carefully and went in and went upstairs to bed. I'd forgotten all about the bear and everything, and I didn't think of it again until the next morning, which came almost right away.

# 4

I HOED POTATOES in our garden all that morning, which was even hotter than it had been the day before. That is, I hoed between doing errands for Mom and Dad. First I hoed potatoes, then I picked a kettle of long green beans for Mom, because we were going to have pork and beans for dinner. You know, hungry boys and hungry bears like pork.

Then I hoed potatoes and took care of Charlotte Ann, and hoed potatoes and carried a drink of water to Dad who was out in the field plowing corn. Then I hoed potatoes. About ten o'clock I went over to Poetry's house to take a note to his mother. You see, the women of our church were having some kind of missionary meeting at our house in the afternoon. Poetry's telephone was out of order and Mom wanted Mrs. Thompson to bring something for lunch, some sandwiches, I think it was.

I didn't feel at all sad about leaving those potatoes although I knew I'd have to finish them sometime. Although there's something very fascinating about cutting out the ugly little weeds and loosening the rich, brown soil and pulling it up nice and fresh around the potato plants. I think maybe it was the fact that my mind was on the bear and a lot of other things, that made me especially glad when I was asked to go over to Poetry's house.

"May I stay and play awhile?" I asked Mom.

"I'm sorry," she said, "not this morning. I have a lot of errands for you, so hurry right back." Then she saw how disappointed I was, so she said, "Well, just thirty minutes, no longer."

I jumped on my bicycle and pedaled down the road as fast as I could to Poetry's. I had to pass Little Jim's house on the way, so I stopped for a minute to rest in the shade of a big cottonwood tree near their front gate. It was Little

Jim's practice time and I could hear him going over and over a certain hard piece of music. I felt sorry for him having to practice on such a hot day, but I knew he was learning something; and you'll never be anybody worthwhile in this world unless you stick to a thing and work hard, whether you want to or not.

Just as I started to go on to Poetry's house, Little Jim's mother came to their front door and called, "Good morning, Bill!"

"Good morning, Mrs. Foote!" I said and tipped my straw hat. A boy would feel like tipping his hat to Little Jim's mother anyway, even if he didn't know it was the right etiquette to tip his hat whenever a lady speaks to him. She was that kind of a woman.

Just that minute, Little Jim began to play one of the church hymns, and it was "Just as I Am."

Pretty soon I was at Poetry's. I gave the note to his mother and she thanked me. And the very first thing she did was to make me sit down and eat a great big piece of warm blackberry pie, which she had just baked. Poetry's mother wasn't small and pretty like Jim's mother and she had big hands and feet, but she had a good mother face, and she liked boys.

Poetry came in from their blackberry patch in time to eat a piece of pie too. Then I went out with him and helped him until we'd picked a whole two-gallon pail of luscious blackberries, each one of us eating maybe a half pint of berries while we were picking.

"Do you know that bears like blackberries?" I asked Poetry, then I let out a low, fierce growl right behind him and grabbed him by the foot and got kicked in the chin as a reward for scaring him. We'd have had a real scuffle if there hadn't been so many briars around.

That started us to telling about bears and I told him what my dad had said about some of our pigs being gone. We just talked and felt scared and brave at the same time, saying what we'd do if a bear came shuffling along right that minute.

"I'd throw this pailful of berries at him," Poetry said, "and then I'd run, and he'd stop to eat the berries, 'cause bears like blackberries better'n barefoot boys." He grinned at all the letter *b*'s he'd used, then he started to say:

Blessing on thee, little man,
  Barefoot boy, with cheek of tan,
 With thy turned-up pantaloons
   And thy merry whistled tunes.

"Do you suppose what you found yesterday was from a real bear?" I asked.

"Naw, it was rabbit's fur. I was just fooling."

Well, it began to look as if the idea of a bear being in our neighborhood was crazy, so we started talking about something else. Although I still believed there might be one, and I made up my mind to find out. Maybe the gang could go down along the swamp that very afternoon, I thought, for we'd planned to go swimming at two o'clock if we could.

Do you know I forgot all about not staying longer than a half hour? I know that's no excuse, but I did forget and I didn't do it on purpose.

After we'd given the pail of berries to his mother, we went out to his tent under the big maple tree. "There's something I want to show you," Poetry said.

I mentioned before that all of the gang were collecting shells that summer. Well, Circus had maybe the best collection of all of us except Little Jim. Of course there wasn't a very large variety of shells to be found along Sugar Creek, but we had relatives that lived in different places and they sent shells to us.

Poetry had an orange scallop, two and one half inches high; and a reddish-brown scallop six inches high, which his uncle had sent him from the Atlantic Ocean; and a knobbed whelk, which is shaped like a pear, from Texas; and a little moon shell and a periwinkle and a greenish-brown squaw-foot and a greenish-black washboard. I had a lot of washboards myself 'cause there were hundreds of them in the riffles in Sugar Creek, and sometimes there are pearls in them.

We had to memorize the poem "The Chambered Nautilus" in school last year. The pearly nautilus is a big snail or a mollusk that crawls on the bottom of the ocean in the South Seas, and the chamber is its shell.

"Want to see my new hobby?" Poetry asked. He pulled a big scrapbook out of a desk drawer and began showing me pictures of a lot of important-looking men and women. He had one section of his scrapbook for famous missionaries, another for evangelists, another for pastors, another for Christian writers and evangelistic singers and doctors and even for nurses. He was just beginning to make the collection, but it certainly looked interesting.

All of a sudden Poetry's mother called from the house that dinner was ready. *Dinner!* Think of it! And I was supposed to stay only a half hour!

In about two jiffies I was gone with the wind. When I got home Dad and Mom were sitting at the table eating. They hadn't even waited for me.

"Hello!" I said cheerfully, being especially careful not to forget to wash my face and comb my hair. Then, to keep them from being disgusted with me, I began telling them all about Poetry's new hobby.

But do you know what? My folks never said a word. Everything was so quiet and I had the strangest feeling inside. When I looked at Dad, he just kept his face straight with his big blackish-red eyebrows half up and half down; and Mom looked sad.

"What's the matter?" I asked innocently. "Is little Charlotte Ann sick or something?"

"Charlotte Ann's all right!" Dad said.

It was a rule in our house not to talk about anything unpleasant at the table, so we didn't; but just the same, I didn't like the atmosphere.

It was a good dinner: pork and beans and bread and butter and blackberry pie.

"I'm sorry," Mom said when it came time for the dessert, "but we've done everything we can to help you not to be forgetful, none of which seem to do any good. Your father and I have decided not to scold you or give you a licking this time. You are not generally disobedient, but you are very thoughtless. So to help you remember, we're asking you to leave the table now without eating any dessert." Her voice was very sad, and so was her face.

I had had my mouth all set for that blackberry pie, liking it maybe better than anything else. Anyway, I did right that minute. So when she said that, all of a sudden something in me turned as hot as fire and I started to talk back. I don't know what made me do it. I knew it was wrong all the time, but I was so mad.

Dad's eyebrows dropped low and his jaw set and he said, "You're excused, William Jasper Collins," which was the name I hated.

I shut up like a washboard clam shuts up down along Sugar Creek when you start to touch it. Then I said, "I don't want any old pie anyway!" I didn't tell them I'd had some at Poetry's house or they wouldn't have thought it was good punishment. I left the table and went into the bathroom to wash my hands, like you're supposed to do after eating.

"Furthermore," Dad said, "you're going to remember to shut the gate from now on, so the pigs won't get out!"

"And you're going to be a little more cheerful about helping me around the house," Mom said.

"And you're *not* going swimming this afternoon!" Dad's big voice thundered.

I went outdoors without saying anything. I knew they were right. I didn't obey very well and I wasn't always cheerful when I did. I knew it was a sin to talk back to my parents and it wasn't right to be so forgetful all the time, 'cause being thoughtless is the same as being selfish and selfishness is sin. On top of that I was supposed to be a Christian. In fact, I was, but I certainly didn't always act like it.

I was so disgusted I picked up a rock and threw it at our old red rooster. And would you believe it? That old rooster got in the way and the rock hit him and broke his leg, and we had to have chicken for dinner the next day.

That only made matters worse. I went out to the barn and climbed up into our haymow. Old Mixy cat was up there, and I yelled, "Scat" at her. She jumped like she was shot and scooted across the hay and down the ladder. Then I threw myself down on the hay and cried and felt sad and wished I'd run away and never come home again. I even wished I was dead.

All of a sudden I felt something hard under my hip, in my pocket. I took it out to see what it was, and it was my little black leather New Testament. I sat there looking at it, and the next thing I knew I was terribly sorry and I got to thinking maybe God still liked me. So I kind of half cried the whole story to Him and asked Him to please do something about Bill Collins being so stubborn and forgetful.

# 5

It was Little Jim who helped me fix things up with my dad. Mom forgave me right away without my even asking her when I went into the house and started helping her; but whenever I looked at Dad he looked the other way or straight in front of him.

It hurt terribly not to be able to go swimming with the gang, but it hurt worse not to have my dad like me anymore.

Along about a quarter after two, when I was out in the garden hoeing, feeling sad and with the dust getting all mixed up with my tears, Little Jim came along. The gang had sent him up from the spring to see why I hadn't come, or if I was sick or something, which I wasn't.

I had to tell somebody so I told Little Jim all about it. He felt very sorry for me. He stood there digging his bare toes into the ground and scooping up little piles of dirt on the back of his foot and kicking them across the garden while I talked. Every now and then he'd stoop and pull a weed to let me know he sympathized with me.

Then he told me the best story and it gave me an idea how I could get my dad to like me again. You see, Little Jim's mom knew all about the famous musicians and she told him interesting stories about different ones.

"Why don't you do what Walter Damrosch did once when he wanted his father to forgive him for something wrong he'd done?" Little Jim asked.

Walter Damrosch, you know, was once the director of the New York Symphony Orchestra and wrote a famous opera called *The Scarlet Letter*. Little Jim's mom had taught him a lot of things like that.

Well, one day when Walter was a little boy and had had a licking for being naughty, he wanted to ask his father to forgive him. But he was afraid to, so he drew a sad picture of himself standing at his father's door. Underneath he'd printed the words "Seventy Times Seven, Shalt Thou Forgive." Then he shoved it under the door of the room where his father was and waited; and pretty soon his dad came out and everything was all right.

I guess you know the Bible story of how Peter once asked the Lord how many times we ought to forgive anybody who sinned against us. "Seven times?" Peter asked. And Jesus said, "Not seven, but seventy times seven."

Well, Little Jim told me the story and it made me feel better so I decided to try it.

"What'll I tell the gang?" Little Jim wanted to know. "They told me to hurry right back."

"Tell them I have to work," I said.

Little Jim started to run back to the gang. Then he stopped and said, "Circus seems awful happy today. I—I'm glad he's saved, aren't you? It just makes me feel all clean inside, kind of like a jackrabbit running through the woods." Then that little fellow tumbled over the fence and away he ran, looking like a jackrabbit himself as he galloped back to the gang.

I sighed a great big sigh and looked out across the green cornfield to where Dad was plowing and wished I was right up on the seat beside him.

*I'll bet he's thirsty*, I said to myself. So I went to the house and got a small jug of water and a pencil and paper.

The picture I drew of myself was sad all right, only it looked more like a lonesome cow than it did me. I wrote at the bottom the words "Seventy times seven," punched a hole through the paper and, with a piece of string, tied it to the handle of the water jug. Then I went through the gate and down to the field where Dad was working and waited for him to get to the end of the row.

The corn was almost knee high already and this was only the first of July. Even the corn looked sad, I thought, and we needed a good rain. All the ends of the blades were rolled because of the heat, and there was a big cloud of dust almost hiding my dad and the team of horses and the plow.

The nearer he came to the end of the row, the

faster my heart beat, and it seemed as if it would burst for hurting me so much.

Pretty soon he stopped the horses, and I ran down between the corn rows and handed him the jug of water with the note tied to it. "Maybe you're thirsty," I said, not looking up at him. As soon as he had the jug in his hand, I turned and ran as fast as I could toward the barn. When I got inside I looked back and watched him through a crack in the door, my heart beating and hurting like everything. I even prayed, "Please, make him forgive me!"

Then I walked through the barn and out another door and went back to hoeing potatoes just as hard as I could, with my back to the cornfield so I couldn't see. I was singing:

Nearer my God to Thee, nearer to Thee. . . .

I changed one part of the chorus and sang:

Still all my soul should be,
Nearer my God to Thee

Pretty soon, in about ten minutes maybe, I heard somebody coming. But I didn't stop to look up. Instead my heart beat faster and faster and I didn't even turn around. Then somebody called my name. But it was Mom's voice and she told me it was too hot to work so fast and that I ought to rest awhile.

But I didn't feel like resting. I looked across the field to where Dad was, and he was plowing away just as if I hadn't given him the note. *Maybe he didn't even see it,* I thought, *or maybe he doesn't care. Maybe he won't ever like me again.*

Pretty soon Mom said, "I'd like to have a pail of cold spring water for making iced tea for the Missionary Circle."

I'd forgotten all about the meeting. I looked quick to see if there were any cars out in front of our house, and there weren't, but I knew they'd be coming soon.

I took our big gallon thermos jug and went through the woods to the spring, hoping none of the gang would be there 'cause I didn't want them to see how sad I felt. But no one was there.

I filled the jug up to the top and let it stand awhile so the jug itself would get cool. In a few minutes I'd pour out the water and fill it again and take it back to Mom.

While I waited I went down to the creek and looked at the lazy little bubble clusters called foam, which floated on the surface. Sugar Creek looked lazy and very sad. In fact, everything looked sad. The whole world needed rain, I thought. Just that minute a rain crow started crying, Kow-kow-kow-kuk-kuk. Rain crows nearly always make the most noise when the weather is cloudy or wet, but maybe he felt sad too, like there were clouds inside of him. He certainly sounded unhappy.

I picked up a flat rock and skipped it across the creek. It struck the water with a splash, made a big leap and then actually skidded on top of the water all the rest of the way across. The waves it made looked kind of like a boy's sad face breaking into a smile. That was the first time I'd ever thought about old Sugar Creek smiling, but he did just the same.

I started to pick up another rock when I happened to think of the rock I'd thrown at our old red rooster, so I dropped it, disgusted.

Four cars were parked in front of our house when I came back with the spring water. I didn't want anybody to see me, so I set the jug down on our kitchen table and hurried out to the garden and started hoeing potatoes again just as my dad came in from the field.

Dad went straight to the toolhouse and got a hoe, and in a jiffy we were hoeing side by side, neither one of us saying anything.

Pretty soon Dad said, "Thank you, Bill, for bringing me a drink. That was very thoughtful of you."

I kept on hoeing, not saying anything. Then I looked up quick and there were actual tears in Dad's eyes, and the next thing I knew I'd made a dive for him almost like a football player makes a tackle, only it was around his neck instead.

Well, I won't tell you what happened just then, but I'll bet I felt even better than the prodigal son did in the Bible when his father hugged him and kissed him, and everything was all right between them.

Then my dad told me something every Christian in the world ought to know, and that is, that the very minute you know you've done something wrong, you ought to be sorry for it. And if you confess it to God real quick, He'll forgive you right that minute, and the blood of Jesus'll wash your heart cleaner than the best soap in the world can wash a boy's dirty hands. But be sure to confess your sin right away.

When Dad had gone back to the field again, it seemed like it was the most wonderful thing in the world to be alive, and I actually liked to hoe potatoes.

The sky was the prettiest blue you ever saw; the heat waves dancing above the corn seemed like they were a lot of happy boys dancing for joy or else like waves splashing in Sugar Creek when you're in swimming. And from away across the field I could hear somebody whistling a cheery tune, and it was my great big dad whistling "Home, Sweet Home." Even though I knew he couldn't hear me, I started whistling the same tune with him, and it was the happiest duet I'd ever whistled in my whole life.

# 6

THAT NIGHT we lost another pig and I knew something would have to be done about it. That afternoon the gang had planned to go up into the hills to see Old Man Paddler, so we decided to go through the swamp instead of going around it as we usually did. We knew about a mulberry tree not far from Old Man Paddler's cabin where there were luscious, thumb-size mulberries just waiting for a boy to climb the tree and pick them.

Old Man Paddler, you know, was a very rich, long-whiskered, kind man who had just come back from a trip around the world. He lived up in the hills alone and liked boys and got lonesome when we didn't come up to see him.

As usual when our gang was together, we sounded like a lot of blackbirds as well as a whole zooful of monkeys. We trudged along, taking turns walking and running and playing leapfrog and rolling in the grass. I had my binoculars along, fastened to a strap around my neck. Poetry was puffing like he always is, 'cause he's so fat. Circus was just the same old Circus except that he seemed to like Little Jim better than ever, and I noticed that in his pocket he had a little New Testament which our pastor had given him the night he was saved.

All of us boys were learning to carry New Testaments so that when we grew up we'd have one in our pockets instead of a package of stinking old cigarettes. Poetry's dad figured it up one day and he actually saved two hundred dollars a year by not smoking, so he sent two hundred dollars every year to help support a national missionary in Africa. Just think of all the saved people that'll be in heaven because of that.

We stopped to rest at the old sycamore tree and to talk about different things. So many important things had happened there. Just then Dragonfly started acting mysterious, and all of a sudden he started climbing the tree. He couldn't climb nearly as fast as Circus and it was a hard tree to climb, but pretty soon he reached the first limb. Nobody was paying any attention to him except me, but I thought he had the strangest expression on his face. All the rest of us talked and chattered, and tumbled over each other in the grass. Pretty soon I heard Dragonfly grunt, and all of a sudden he came sliding down the tree with that same look on his face and for a minute there was an expression in his eye like Old Man Paddler has sometimes.

Then Dragonfly began playing and acting like the rest of us.

All the way through the swamp I kept thinking about bears and using my binoculars to see if I could see one. When we came to the place where Dragonfly had seen the big black hog wallowing in the mud—if it was a hog—we all stopped and examined the ground carefully to see if there were any bear tracks. But there weren't, that is, we didn't see any and nothing had been there since the other time. Just the same, I sighed when we came out on the other side of the swamp and started to climb the hill toward Old Man Paddler's cabin.

In about twenty minutes we were there. It was an old log cabin, looking kind of like the picture of the cabin Abraham Lincoln was born in. We stopped at the spring where the old man gets his drinking water, each one of us taking turns drinking, lying down on our stomachs and drinking like cows.

Pretty soon we saw the old man, standing in the doorway with his long white whiskers reaching down almost to his waist. He had so many whiskers you couldn't tell whether he was smiling. You had to look into his eyes to find that out, but he always had a twinkle in those eyes when he saw a boy.

That kind old man invited us in and made us drink sassafras tea like he always does when we go to see him. While we were sitting around listening to him tell us stories—some of us were sitting on chairs and some on the floor—he surprised us by saying something that made us feel very sad. "Boys," he said in his trembling old voice, "I'm not going to live very much longer in this world. Last week I went to town and made a will, and in that will I left something for each one of you. I haven't forgotten that it was you who saved my life a month ago, and my money too."

Little Jim looked away quick 'cause he always liked old people so well, and especially Old Man Paddler.

None of us knew what to say. But finally Big Jim cleared his throat and said courteously, "Thank you, Mr. Paddler. We're glad we had a chance to be your friends. You've helped us boys a great deal."

Then the old man stood up and said, "I must be getting on with my work now. Be sure to come again soon."

He didn't tell us what his work was, and we didn't ask, but we were all curious. We went outdoors and down to the spring for another drink.

When Little Jim had had his drink, I noticed he had tears in his eyes. While we were on our way up to the mulberry tree, he and I walked together, and I asked, "What's the matter?"

He took a hard swish at a big bull thistle with his stick before he answered, "I don't *want*

Old Man Paddler to die!" And I didn't either. Of course, I couldn't help wondering what he'd planned to give us, but I didn't like to think about it; it didn't seem right to. There wasn't a one of our gang that even mentioned it, 'cause we all liked the old man so well we wanted him to keep right on living forever.

I forgot to tell you that's what Big Jim said to him back there in the cabin. Can you guess what the old man answered him? He said, "Live forever?" and kind of laughed. "That's exactly what I'm going to do, only I'm going to move out of this dilapidated old house first." And I knew he didn't mean his weathered old log cabin with its clapboard roof, but a wrinkled, white-haired old house with long white whiskers and gnarled old hands that trembled.

In a few minutes we were all up in the mulberry tree, each boy on a limb, gobbling up whole handfuls of the juiciest, biggest, blackest mulberries you ever saw.

When we'd eaten all we could, we started back toward home. We'd stayed a little longer than we should have, I guess, because with the tall trees making so much shade, it was kind of spooky in the old swamp. But we decided to go through anyway because it was so much closer.

Then, just like it had happened that other afternoon, it happened again. We heard a heavy, crashing noise like something big was running away. We stopped dead in our tracks.

Then we heard a fierce growl, and in a jiffy something charged right past us so close it almost ran into us. We heard dogs barking fiercely and running after whatever it was that was running away. We started to run!

Gasping, panting, scared half to death, we came out into the open on the other side of the swamp and we didn't stop running until we reached the spring.

That was the second time we'd seen it, whatever it was. Circus said it was his dad's big hounds chasing a rabbit; Big Jim said it might have been a fox but that it was the dogs that made all the noise; Little Jim sighed and believed Big Jim; Poetry said whatever it was, it was a coward 'cause it was always running away; Dragonfly said he'd seen it clearly and that it weighed five hundred pounds and was black and had long hair and its eyes were small and brown—or maybe gray.

We all tried to believe Big Jim for he was nearly always right. None of us believed it was a bear, and we couldn't always trust Dragonfly's eyes. They saw so many things that just weren't. So I said, "I think it had purple eyes with yellow stripes in them."

That made us all laugh and we got over being scared almost right away.

Just then we heard a shot behind us, and we all jumped. Then there was another shot.

"It's my dad," Circus said. And in a minute Circus' dad came swinging along toward us, carrying his gun in one hand and a squirrel in the other. His two big dogs were running along beside him with their long tongues hanging out and panting and looking happy and satisfied, just like a boy looks after he's been in swimming or won a baseball game or something. Even though I felt sorry for the squirrel, I felt glad because I knew the Brownes would have something to eat for supper. Circus' mother liked squirrel soup better than anything else in the world, Circus told me once.

"Hello, boys!" Circus' dad said cheerfully.

"Hello," we said. The last time I'd seen him was when he was on his knees in the big brown tent with my dad's arm around him.

Then he said to Circus, "I guess we'd better run along home now, son, and get the chores done and supper over. Your mom wants to go to the meeting tonight."

I looked at Little Jim and he looked at me, and Dragonfly kind of hung his head. He was the only one of our gang now that wasn't born again, I thought. He'd gone with us to the tent meetings several times but he didn't seem to understand things.

On the way home, Dragonfly said to me and Little Jim who were walking and running and playing leapfrog together, "What do they do to you when you go forward in the tent?" Imagine him saying that!

"Nothing," Little Jim said. "You just make up your mind you want to be saved and you invite Jesus into your heart. The minister or somebody who knows, shows what it says in the Bible and you just tell Jesus you're a sinner and that you believe He died on the cross for you and that you receive Him as your Saviour right now."

Dragonfly looked serious a minute, then he jumped over Little Jim like a jackrabbit over a log and said, "I've told Him that already."

"When?" I asked.

"About two hours ago when I was sliding down out of the old sycamore tree, like Zaccheus did in the Bible."

Just then Circus, who didn't know what we were talking about, came running toward us like he was a savage, wild animal, and in a jiffy we were all tumbling over each other on the grass like puppies playing, and we didn't get to say anything more to Dragonfly.

Just before we parted at my house, however, I saw Dragonfly ask Little Jim something which I couldn't hear. Then he started running down the road as fast as he could with Little Jim right at his heels.

# 7

WELL, IT BEGAN TO LOOK as if the idea of a bear being in our neighborhood was only my imagination because I had been reading about bears in my dad's library, and was just hoping there was one there. Dad found a big hole in the fence where the pigs had been getting out. The only thing was that two of the pigs never came back in, and none of the neighbors had seen them.

The gang didn't get to meet again until the last of that week, 'cause it was harvesttime and we had to cut oats.

I was always glad when a lot of men were working for us because they always stayed for dinner and that meant that we'd have the best dinners in the world—pie and cake and fried chicken, which was a favorite dish. And it wouldn't be any old red rooster either, but young spring chicken. I never did eat any chicken that was tougher than our old red rooster, and for some reason I didn't enjoy it very much.

Dad hired Circus' dad and Circus and a strange man to help us with the work. The strange man had a hooked nose, with a puffy face and pig eyes and looked like he drank whiskey. He had just moved into the neighborhood and lived on the other side of Sugar Creek and needed work. He had two rough boys who hadn't been to Sunday school in their whole lives, although they'd lived in towns where there were plenty of churches.

Dad hitched four horses to our binder, or harvester, as they call it in our school books, and pretty soon there was a happy humming and roaring of machinery and the fun began. It was hard work, but we liked it. Circus and I did almost as much work as his dad and the strange man, whose name was John Till.

We became hot and tired and sweaty and felt like real men. Dad had hired me too, and was going to pay me as much as he would have paid anybody else.

Circus seemed a little worried though, for every now and then he would look over at his dad and the strange man as if he were afraid of something. "What's the matter?" I asked.

He said, "Nothing, only Dad used to know John Till before he was saved."

Circus kept on watching his dad, and every now and then I could see him looking disgusted at John Till.

Once Circus stopped and said to me, "See that big bulge in John Till's hip pocket?"

"What is it?" I asked.

"Whiskey," Circus said and wiped the sweat off his face and started in working harder than ever.

Everything went along all right until about three o'clock in the afternoon when Circus' dad and the strange man stopped for a while and went over to a little bunch of elderberry bushes along the fence where we kept the water jug.

From where we were, we could see the men taking turns drinking out of the jug like working men do, pouring out a little water before and after drinking, so the next man won't get any of his germs if he has any.

Just that minute Circus let out a yell and started running across the field toward them and screaming, "Stop! Don't you dare give him that whiskey!" My dad was away across on the other side of the field.

I felt the blood start racing in my veins and my heart pounding, and in a jiffy I was running as fast as I could right after Circus. The sweat was pouring down my face and getting into my eyes and I could hardly see. My hat blew off. I could see Circus ahead of me, running like I'd never seen him run in all my life.

I knew how much Circus' dad used to like whiskey and, even though he had been saved last Monday night, he might yield to temptation and drink again. Circus knew it too.

Already we were too late. I saw Circus' dad take the bottle from the hook-nosed man and lift it to his lips. And just that minute Circus got there, with me right at his heels. I never saw Circus so mad in my life, and I remembered that night in my room when he had looked so fierce and had said what he did about the old whiskey advertising.

Circus let out a yell and made a leap for the bottle, trying to get it away from his dad and screaming, *"Don't, Dad! You're supposed to be a Christian!"*

But John Till's big arm shot out and his rough, hard hand grabbed Circus' shirt collar, and he whirled him around like a giant would a little toy and shoved him back. And Circus' dad took another drink.

Then my red-haired temper caught fire and I couldn't even see; I was so mad at John Till and the devil and whiskey and sin. I made a fierce dive for that man with both fists flying; and even though I couldn't see anything but his pig eyes and hooked nose and my flying fists, I could feel my fist striking the man's nose and chin and stomach.

Then something struck me on the jaw and things began to whirl around and around, and I fell flat to the ground. That was the last I knew for a while.

When I came to, I was lying in the shade of the elderberry bushes. I could smell the sweet perfume of the big white clusters of flowers. Circus was sitting in the shade beside me, holding a sore knuckle to his lips.

Circus' dad was there too, crying, and I heard my dad's big voice say angrily, talking to the hook-nosed man, *"You're fired!* Here's your money, and don't ever set foot on my farm again until you can act like a human being!"

Then my dad cut loose with the grandest sermon against whiskey you ever heard, saying that if it was right to sell or drink it, it was also right to kill people by running into them with automobiles or actually murdering them on purpose 'cause when people were drunk they couldn't drive straight and you never could tell when a drinking man was going to lose control of himself and kill somebody.

"You great big whiskey guzzler!" my dad thundered. "Here's a father who is trying to go straight, who's given his heart and life to God and is trying to be a Christian! And you try to get him to go back and join the devil's army. Don't you have any respect for decency and law and order? Don't you have any respect for the man's children who need a Christian father and what money he can earn for food and clothing? Don't you know, John Till, that *some day you've got to stand before the judgment bar of almighty God? And that the wages of sin is death?*"

Boy! I felt proud of my dad!

He gave the man a full day's pay and sent him home.

Well, that was our introduction to the Till family. You can see how John Till's two rough boys wouldn't like the Sugar Creek Gang very well. The Till boys' names were Bob and Tom. We found out afterward that they were named after Bob Ingersoll and Tom Paine, whom you'll hear more about when you grow up. My dad says Bob Ingersoll was an atheist which means he didn't believe there is a God; and Tom Paine was a deist, which means he didn't believe the Bible is God's Word.

John Till was an atheist himself, and he certainly acted like it. Circus' dad was very sorry about yielding to temptation and he asked my dad to forgive him, which my dad did. He said

when he saw the bottle of whiskey he felt a terrible burning in his throat and he wanted it so
bad that it seemed he'd go crazy if he didn't have
it. That's what liquor does to a man when it
gets hold of him. That's why a boy or anybody
shouldn't take even one little tiny drink, because
one drink is the devil's bait to get you to walk
into his trap.

Well, Dad and Circus and I and Circus' dad
were all Christians, so my dad said, "Let's have
a little prayer meeting right here and pray for
John Till and for each other and ask God to
give Dan here strength to say no next time."

In a jiffy we were all down on our knees in
the shade of the elderberry bushes, with the
sweet-smelling flowers all around us and with
crickets cheeping in the grass and the hot wind
blowing and rustling the leaves, and with a
great big lump of ache in our hearts.

We took turns praying. I can't remember
what I said. But whatever it was, I meant it,
even if I didn't know how to pray very well.
It was a grand prayer meeting and I'll bet God
looked down at us and liked us better than ever
for having it out there under the little elder-

berry bushes which He made to grow there. Maybe He'd put them there on purpose, He liking His people so well.

# 8

IF I DON'T WATCH OUT I'll get to the end of this story without telling you how Little Jim killed the bear. But I have to explain all these other things first 'cause they're what is called the setting of the story. Also, I'll have to tell you something about Bob and Tom Till, because they're in the story too, Tom especially. Besides, the bear isn't the only important thing in this book, not by a long shot.

Bob was fourteen years old and was as big as Big Jim, bigger, in fact. He had even shaved his moustache once or twice. Tom had red hair like mine and was as mean as anything. The first time we saw the boys was one day about a week after my dad had fired their dad for giving whiskey to Circus' dad.

Our gang had been in swimming and having a great time and we were out in the shade of a big peach-leaf willow tree dressing when we heard somebody laughing up in the woods. Well, after swimming, we'd planned to go up on the hill near the big rock where we knew there were a lot of ripe wild strawberries just waiting for hungry boys to come and pick them.

We'd been the only boys in our neighborhood for a long time, and it seemed as if the strawberries and the creek and all the woods belonged to us. The fact is, they belonged to Old Man Paddler, and he'd given us permission to pick strawberries or do anything we wanted to there.

"It's the Till boys," Dragonfly said. "They're up there eating our strawberries."

We dressed in a hurry and started on the run through the woods. Then we sneaked up behind some bushes and watched them. But there weren't only two Till boys; there were four or five other boys who lived in town and belonged to a tough gang, the same gang the Till boys had belonged to before they'd moved into the country.

They were just gobbling up our strawberries as fast as they could and laughing and hollering to each other and swearing and saying nasty things which none of our gang ever said because Big Jim wouldn't stand for it, and because it was wrong.

I think it was their swearing that made us disgusted more than it was the fact that they were eating our strawberries. They were all barefoot, but none of them looked like the boy in the poem we'd learned in school, which says:

> Blessings on thee, little man,
>   Barefoot boy with cheek of tan;
>
> .    .    .    .    .    .    .
>
> With thy red lips, redder still,
>   Kissed by strawberries on the hill.

None of our gang felt like a poem either. We just lay there watching, with our tempers like fuses burning shorter and shorter toward a half-dozen sticks of dynamite, each one expecting to explode any minute.

Little Jim's fists were all doubled up 'cause he couldn't stand to hear anybody swear. And before any of us knew what he was going to do, he darted out into the open and yelled, "You boys stop that swearing!" Then he ducked into the bushes and crouched down beside Big Jim.

Well, that started the thing, that is, started their fuses to burning too. There wasn't any use to stay hidden, so Big Jim gave the signal and we all stepped out to where they could see us.

There wasn't a one of us who didn't think we could lick those boys, but Big Jim didn't want us to fight unless we had to.

As soon as they saw us, they knew who we were. I guess nearly everybody in the whole country had heard about us.

Big Jim had his hat pulled down low over one eye and looked pretty fierce. I could see he had his eye on the biggest Till boy and was figuring how easy it would be to lick him.

Getting ready to fight is a funny thing. You feel scared and angry and afraid all at the same time, and yet you aren't really scared; and you can't even see straight for wanting to punch the other fellow's nose.

As I told you, they knew who we were and

didn't like us. You see, when a boy gets about half grownup and doesn't go to Sunday school or church, he thinks every boy who does go, is a sissy. Anyway the Till boys' dad must have seen us having that meeting under the elderberry bushes, 'cause just then the littlest one called out to us, "Hello, there! You prayer-meeting sissies!"

I felt sorry for those boys for being so ignorant, but just the same it didn't feel very good to be called that. I could tell that my fuse was just about burned to the end.

"We're not sissies!" Dragonfly shouted back.

I looked at Poetry to see how he felt and his face was as red as a beet. "Those are *our* strawberries!" he yelled at them.

"Oh they are, are they?" Big Bob Till called back. "If they are, why don't you come and get them!" Then he said sarcastically, "We extend to you a cordial invitation to come up and help yourselves. Or maybe you believe in praying for them!"

We all waited for Big Jim to decide what to do. I'd already decided which one of the boys I was going to fight, if I had to.

Pretty soon Big Jim said to us, "You boys wait here a minute." Then he stepped out and marched right up the hill toward them. His voice was shaking, he was so angry, and I knew he was just itching to sock that big bully in the jaw. Instead, he made the grandest speech. He said, "Fellows, it isn't a question of whether we're afraid to fight. There isn't a man among us that's got a drop of coward's blood in him. But the Sugar Creek Gang doesn't believe in fighting, and we won't unless we have to.

"We have permission from the owner of the woods to pick strawberries here, and we ask you if you will please leave and not make it necessary for us to use force."

*That,* I said to myself, *is self-control, the kind Bill Collins needs.* I felt proud of Big Jim.

But Big Bob Till just looked disgusted. "You're a bunch of Sunday school and prayer-meeting sissies!" he shouted back. "You're afraid to fight!" He took a step toward Big Jim with his fists all doubled up. Then he turned around to his gang and said, "Come on, gang, let's lick the daylights out of them!"

And just like a swarm of angry bumblebees,

the gang of boys charged down the hill at us, with their fists flying and their mouths spilling nasty words and calling us all kinds of filthy names.

Now, I ask you, what's a fellow going to do when he knows he shouldn't fight but when the other fellow needs a licking more than he needs anything else? Many a time I'd needed a licking myself and my dad had given it to me and it had done me good. So I made up my mind quicker'n a lightning flash that since that mean-faced, red-haired Till boy, who was just my size, needed a licking, I was going to give it to him.

That's all the thinking I got to do, 'cause when you're in a fight you can't think very well. I'm telling you that was a real battle; and while we were in it, it seemed more important than Waterloo or the Marne or Gettysburg or any other famous battle.

The first thing I knew was that little red-haired fellow smacked me on the side of the nose and made me grunt; and that was the last of my fuse. Also, that's how hoeing potatoes and doing a lot of hard farm work came in handy. My muscles felt like the blacksmith's

89

whose smithy stands under the spreading chestnut tree.

It was Little Jim who surprised us the most. Once between blows, I saw him down on top of another little fellow about his size and he had that other kid by the wrists and was yelling down into his face, "Don't you know it's *wrong* to swear? Don't you know Jesus is your best Friend?"

And would you believe it? Little Jim just yelled down the grandest sermon you ever heard into that little fellow's face.

Just then I made a quick dive for Tom Till's knees, and he went down like a football player does when he's tackled. Poetry and the boy he was fighting, stumbled over us and came down kersquawsh right on top of us with Poetry on top of the pile, with our arms and legs getting all tangled up. If anybody had seen us just then, he couldn't have told which one of us any of those eight dirty, bare feet belonged to.

Getting hit doesn't hurt very much when you're in a fight, and I didn't even know I had a black eye until afterward. I thought the reason I couldn't see very well was 'cause I was so mad.

Poetry was fighting like he actually enjoyed it. All of a sudden I heard him quoting a poem about the village blacksmith, one which we'd had to learn in school. He had his man down and was sitting on him and yelling:

> Under a spreading chestnut-tree
>   The village smithy stands;
> The smith, a mighty man is he,
>   With large and sinewy hands;
> And the muscles of his brawny arm,
>   Are strong as iron bands.

And then Poetry just yelled it out:

> He goes on Sunday to the church!

He said it over and over again, *"He goes on Sunday to the church! He goes on Sunday to the church!"* And every time he gave his man another blow he said, "He goes on Sunday to the church!"

There wasn't a one of our gang that was ashamed of going to church. We knew if *anybody* is a sissy, it's the boy that's afraid to go to church for fear somebody'll make fun of him!

91

Don't think it was easy to lick those boys, however. Their muscles were as strong as iron bands too, and some of them had had boxing lessons. Dragonfly seemed to be having the hardest time. I looked around once just in time to see somebody's long arm strike out and a big dirty fist struck him right in the nose; and that was the last of Dragonfly's fuse too. After that he was like a little wildcat. From then on the Sugar Creek Gang began to make short work of those fellows.

I guess Big Bob Till had never been licked in his life until that day. But then he'd always been a bully and had probably picked on boys smaller than he was. So when our Big Jim, who was fighting a skillful boxing fight and was as cool as a cucumber, licked the stuffin's out of him, it was maybe the best thing that ever happened to him.

Just that minute I heard something buzzing around my head and felt a sharp pain in my arm and over my other eye, and I knew somebody had stirred up a bumblebee's nest. In a jiffy the air was full of black and yellow bumblebees that were madder even than we were.

Those big black and yellow buzzers came storming out of that nest like soldiers out of their dugouts and, before we knew it, we were running to the woods as fast as we could, and the fight was over.

The thing to do if a bee is after you, is to run fast, then suddenly drop flat to the ground and lie still, and that'll lose the bee. He'll go around in circles up above you and, if you wait long enough without moving, he'll go away. But we didn't start running soon enough.

My eye began to swell right away, and before I went to bed that night both my eyes were so swollen I could hardly see a thing.

That didn't end our trouble with the Till boys, even though it was the end of the fight, for that fall we all had to go to the same little red brick schoolhouse together.

# 9

THE FIRST THING I DID when I got home was to slip into our bathroom and lock the door and take a good look at myself in the mirror. Or perhaps I should say, a bad look. I certainly was a sight, and I think I actually looked meaner than the little red-haired, mean-faced Till boy.

I didn't like to have my parents see me like that, but of course they did. I washed my hands and face carefully and combed my hair. When I came out of the bathroom, Mom, who was getting supper, gasped and said, "What on *earth!*"

I hated to mention the fight, so I said, trying to be indifferent, "Oh, I just got too close to a bumblebee who didn't like me very well." I knew that before long I'd have to tell her about the fight though.

Mom stood there with a teakettle in one hand and a potato peeler in the other, and with astonishment all over her face. She said, "It certainly looks like you got too close to two bumblebees!" There was a twinkle in her eyes though. She knew boys pretty well and was used to having me come home with a sore toe or a worn shirt or with a new bump on my head where I'd fallen down somewhere.

Mom turned around and poured water out of the teakettle into something she was cooking, then she said, using the same tone of voice I'd been using, "What were you trying to do? Use the bumblebees for binoculars?"

She didn't scold me for getting stung 'cause she figured maybe I couldn't help it. Besides, getting stung and having your eye swell almost shut, is enough punishment. I certainly would know enough to be careful next time without being told.

I went in to see Charlotte Ann who was getting cuter every day and who had the sweetest smile. We'd do most anything to get her to smile, such as tickling her under the chin or touching her pink toes or making funny faces, and sometimes she wouldn't, but would just lie there with her big blue eyes open wide and look innocent. Then her little arms and legs would start going like four windmills, and she would coo and act awful smart.

Well, when I came in with my swollen eyes, she started smiling right away. "How do you like your big ugly-faced brother?" I asked her, and those four windmills started going and she looked like she was so happy she could talk, only she couldn't.

I picked her up carefully like Mom had taught me to and held her a while, being especially careful to hold her so her little head wouldn't bob around too much. Then we went and stood in front of our big mirror in Mom's bedroom.

I tell you she was a grand little sister. Something in me just bubbled up kind of like the water does down in the spring, and I kissed her on the top of her curly, black head and called her Charlie and said, "We're going to be pals when you grow up, aren't we?"

That bubbling up kept going right on inside of me. Oh, I tell you she was wonderful! Grand! Great! Astonishing! Perfectly swell!

I put Charlie down in her bassinet and went out into the kitchen, gave Mom a hug and went galloping out of doors, yelling "Whoopie!" forgetting all about my swollen eyes, except that I couldn't see very well. I started helping dad with the chores.

"I don't see how you can go to the meeting tonight," Dad said when we were eating supper. "You'll attract more attention than the minister."

I hadn't thought about that, and all of a sudden I wanted to go more than ever. This was the last week of the Good News Crusade, and I didn't want to miss a night. I looked at Dad and suggested, "Maybe I could sit out in front in our car if we can park close enough." That's one thing I liked about having church in a tent in the summertime. So many people who wouldn't go to church at all, would listen outside. Besides, it was cool in the tent at night.

Finally they decided to let me go but said

I'd have to wear dark glasses, which I always liked to do anyway.

Little Jim sat on one side of me and Circus on the other. There were two choirs, one of older people and the other of boys and girls, called the Booster Chorus, and we were in the Booster Chorus.

It was grand, sitting up there on that platform in the big brown tent with hundreds and hundreds of people out in front of us, and with all the ministers sitting behind the evangelist.

Our Booster Chorus platform was away over near the tent's big side walls and I could hear people outside, walking around and talking. All at once I heard a voice I knew. For a minute I forgot all about the meeting, I was so astonished. Would you believe it? It was the voice of that mean-faced Till boy who had smacked me on the side of the nose and given me that black eye.

"Let's go in," I heard him say to somebody.

"Naw!" another voice said. "People'll see us."

"Fraidy cat!" Tom Till said.

"If the gang finds out, they'll make fun of us," the other boy objected.

Then little Tom Till started to say, quoting a line from one of Poetry's poems, "He goes on Sunday to the church. He goes on Sunday to the church," just like Poetry had said it that afternoon to the boy he'd licked.

"Aw, shut up!" the other voice said, and I decided maybe he was the one Poetry had licked.

I didn't hear anything more for a while, but pretty soon the tent's side wall was lifted a little and two boys in overalls crawled in and sat down in the grass behind a big tent pole. One of the boys was the little red-headed Tom Till and the other one was the one Poetry had licked that afternoon.

Say, Tom Till had a black eye like mine and I knew where he'd gotten it.

Those two boys listened like everything and didn't act disgusted with the meeting at all.

Once Little Jim nudged me to let me know he'd seen the boys too. He asked for my ever-sharp pencil and wrote a little note and slipped it to me, and the note said in Little Jim's awkward writing: "I don't hate them anymore. I'm going to pray for them."

For a minute I couldn't see the words because of some crazy tears that got mixed up with my swollen eyes, but I scribbled on the bottom of his note, "Me too," and handed it back to him. He slipped it over to Circus. After all, I decided, Jesus had died for all the red-haired, mean-faced little boys in the world, hadn't He?

I didn't know Circus could sing, but he actually had a beautiful voice. I decided when I heard it that I was going to tell Little Jim's mother, and maybe she'd give him voice lessons free. Maybe I could even take some money out of my bank and pay for them. I could tell by the way Circus was watching the song leader who had the cornet that he was thinking that some day he was going to be an evangelistic singer. Wouldn't that be grand? Maybe Little Jim could be the evangelist, and I'd be a Christian doctor who lived in their town and made a lot of money. I'd help pay the rent on the tent and things.

Out in the main part of the tent, not far from the front, sat Circus' folks. It felt good to see them there, all in a row, with his dad all dressed up and his mom looking happy with their new baby in her lap and three kind of ordinary-looking girls between them. One of the girls was about my age and had wavy brown hair and a nice face. And I thought that maybe when school started next fall, if a boy stood on his head in front of her or walked a rail fence without falling off or killed a spider for her or something she'd smile back at him.

All through the sermon I kept looking down at the little Till boy and thinking how maybe if he'd had my parents he'd have been a different boy, and I felt sorry for him.

After the meeting, Little Jim and I kind of edged over in his direction, but before we could get there, he and the other boy had ducked under the tent and were gone.

# 10

NOW FOR THE BEAR STORY!

I guess you know that if there is anything a bear likes better than pork, it's honey. It even eats bees.

Black bears can climb a tree almost as well as Circus can. Whenever they find a bee tree, they climb right up and get all the honey, if they can. They don't seem to mind getting stung, and they can smell honey a long way off.

Baby bears can climb trees too, that is, black bears. Grizzly bears can't. The first thing a black mother bear does when there's danger, is to make the little bear children climb a tree.

Well, the Sugar Creek Gang liked honey too, bumblebee honey especially; only you have to kill all the bumblebees before you can rob their nest. I know boys shouldn't kill bumblebees, 'cause the red clover which makes such sweet hay for horses and cows and is so good for a farmer's land, couldn't be pollenized without the bumblebees going from flower head to flower head gathering honey and at the same time carrying pollen, which sticks to their legs.

But we didn't know that at first, and besides when you get stung by a bumblebee you can't exactly be expected to like them.

Anyway, the next day we decided to go back and rob that bumblebees' nest. We met at the spring right after dinner and were all there except Poetry and Circus. Circus couldn't come that day because his mother was sick and he didn't think he ought to leave home.

Big Jim had brought his rifle along and it was leaning against a beech tree, in the bark of which we had all carved our initials.

I don't know what there is about a rifle that makes a boy feel like a man when he's carrying one. Big Jim hardly ever had his rifle when we were together, except in the winter when we sometimes went hunting. But when he did, we all begged to be allowed to carry it 'cause it made us feel so important; and we were very, *very* careful the way we carried it, so there wouldn't be any danger to the rest of the gang.

"Circus' mother is pretty sick," Big Jim said, and that made us all feel bad. Then he added, "She likes squirrel soup better than anything else; so if any of you boys see a squirrel be sure to tell me. My mother'll make the soup and take it over to her." Big Jim, you know, lived right across the road from Circus' house.

Maybe I ought to tell you that Dragonfly and Little Jim both owned guns that shoot B-B shots and aren't as dangerous as real guns. Little Jim could shoot almost as straight as Circus whose dad had a lot of guns, and Circus could shoot even better than Big Jim. Sometimes Little Jim had shot Big Jim's rifle too, when we were shooting at targets.

We waited for Poetry and pretty soon he came along, carrying a big brown jug.

"What's the jug for?" we asked.

He just looked mysterious and said, "I'm going to put the bumblebees in it so we can get the honey."

"You're crazy!" Dragonfly said.

But Poetry had a wise look on his face. He went straight to the spring and began filling the jug with water, saying,

> The bees are flying and humming,
> Why are they all coming?
> Honey to seek,
> Honey to seek,
> Bz, bz, Bzzzz.

When the jug was about half full he stopped, straightened up and said, "Now we are ready to go."

So we started, all of us keeping our eyes open for squirrels.

Pretty soon we were at the little border of bushes that skirts the hill where the strawberries are.

"Now you boys wait a minute," Poetry said, "until I get the bees all in the jug."

So we waited, still thinking he was foolish. He took Little Jim's stick in one hand and the jug in the other and crept along like an Indian getting ready to spring upon an enemy.

Once he stopped and turned around and grinned at us and said, "Anybody that wants to, can have fried bumblebees for supper. They make the nicest gravy." Then we knew he was crazy.

In a few jiffies he had found the nest. Quick as a flash he sloshed the jug down right beside it, shoved Little Jim's stick into the middle of the nest, gave the stick a twist or two and came flying down the hill to where we were lying in the bushes.

Those bees came swarming out madder'n anything, dozens of them, hundreds of them it looked like. And would you believe it? They started going into the mouth of that water jug, just tumbling in like a lot of black and yellow Santa Clauses going down a chimney. Of course with all the water in there, they got their wings wet and couldn't get out.

After a while when the bees were all in, we walked up and dug out our honey. Yum! Yum! Was it ever good! We smacked our lips, keeping on the lookout for any stray bees that had been away from home gathering honey. Every now and then one came back disgusted as anything; but when they came one at a time like that, it was easy for us to kill them with our straw hats.

There were a lot of bee cells which had larvae in them, and we had to leave some of the honey which was all mixed up with bees which were in what is called the chrysalis stage. We'd learned about that in school.

Pretty soon we went swimming again. Then, like we'd done the day before, we started back to get the strawberries, wondering if the Till boys would be there again. Just that minute Dragonfly said, "Phsst! There he is!" he cried. "The little red-haired one!"

I looked quick and so did everyone else, but we didn't see anything. Sometimes Dragonfly was wrong, you know. Anyway, he didn't see him again either.

"Maybe they're in our strawberry patch," Dragonfly said, feeling disappointed that he'd been mistaken.

Just to make sure, we sneaked up carefully behind the bushes, and then all of a sudden Dragonfly said, "Phsst!" again.

You could have knocked me over with a dandelion. We all saw it at once—them, rather; for right there where the bumblebees' nest had been was a great big black mother bear and a brown-nosed baby bear! They were eating bee bread and larvae and everything we'd left. The mother had dried mud all over her sides like she'd been wallowing in the swamp.

"It's a *b-bear!*" Dragonfly hissed. *"A sure enough wild bear!"*

# 11

I COULDN'T BELIEVE IT at first—that it was a bear—but I had to. Just that second the little brown-nosed cub must have done something his mother didn't like, 'cause she whirled around and whacked him with her powerful forepaw and sent him tumbling over the grass and down the hill toward us. But he shuffled to his feet and went back for more honey.

"Let's catch him and take him home for a pet," Little Jim said with his eyes wide. I couldn't help but think the same thing.

Pretty soon the mother let out a low growl and stood up on her haunches and sniffed the air suspiciously, like she was saying, "Whoever you are, get out of here 'cause I'm disgusted with you for not leaving more honey."

Of course we didn't interfere with their meal 'cause that's when bears are dangerous—when you interrupt them when they're eating and try to chase them away or something. Even our old Mixy cat gets cross if she's eating a mouse and you try to get close enough to her to pet her. She actually scratched me once.

The wind was blowing down the hill, so we knew they couldn't smell us. Dragonfly suggested, looking at Big Jim's rifle, "How about bear soup? Do you suppose Circus' mother would like that?"

Little Jim's forehead puckered at that, kind of like somebody had stuck him with a pin. It actually hurt him to think of that cute little cub having to be killed.

We lay there, keeping as quiet as possible, thinking and watching Big Jim's face to see what he was going to do. All of a sudden I noticed the little yellow fuzz which had been growing on Big Jim's upper lip was gone. That meant he had shaved it off, and I wished I'd hurry up and grow big enough to shave too. Big Jim was almost a man now, I thought.

We must have made too much noise, for all at once the mother bear sniffed again; then she whirled around and lumbered off toward the woods with the baby bear running close to her, kind of like a baby calf crowding up against a mother cow. That little fellow could hardly keep up, and its awkward little legs looked ridiculous.

But—they were running straight toward us! You can guess we were plenty scared. We scrambled in all directions and started to run away. But when that old bear saw us, she was as surprised as we were. She was running away too and just happened to be running in our direction, not knowing we were there. When she saw so many of us all at once and heard us screaming, she got all mixed up in her mind and didn't know which way to turn.

I don't know how it happened but Big Jim got in the way somehow, and the little bear ran smack into him and knocked him sprawling; and for a minute he and the cub were rolling over and over on the grass.

We decided afterward that if the mother'd been alone, she'd have run away; but when she saw her baby getting all tangled up with Big Jim, suddenly she went mad. She thought Big Jim was trying to hurt her little brown-nosed baby.

She sent that little cub up a tree in a hurry, then she whirled around fiercely with her big teeth flashing and looking strong enough to crush the bones of a cow. They were a whole lot bigger than the teeth of the old wolf who had eaten Little Red Riding Hood's grandmother. Her long-clawed forepaws looked like they could knock a boy flatter than a pancake.

In the scramble Big Jim dropped his rifle. It lay at the foot of the tree, half covered with leaves, and the bear was between us and the gun.

Just that second we heard somebody screaming and, looking up, we saw the little red-haired Till boy up the same tree as the little bear cub. Dragonfly was right after all. Tom Till was holding on for dear life and was crying and scared half to death.

The little bear was sitting on a limb right

114

below him, and the fierce old mother bear was at the foot of the tree, acting like she was going right up after him. I couldn't help but remember last night in the tent, and Little Jim's note. And all at once I liked little Tom Till and didn't want anything to happen to him.

Little Jim was closer to the gun than any of us and, as I told you before, he was very brave even when he was scared. I think I told you in my other story that he was carrying Big Jim's rifle, but he wasn't actually carrying it, not until afterward.

As I told you, that old mother was terribly savage. If Tom Till hadn't been up that tree and in danger, I think our gang would have run away, because it's foolish to trifle with a mad bear. But we didn't dare go away, and we didn't dare stay either. We didn't know what to do.

It seemed that old bear wasn't mad at us though, but at Tom Till who was up the same tree as her baby cub. She whirled around and up onto her haunches and started to climb the tree, which was a red oak and easy to climb.

Just then Little Jim darted in toward the tree and swooped down on the gun. He had his hands on it when she saw him, and as quick as lightning she whirled and made a lunge straight at him.

It was terrible! I screamed and screamed and grabbed a club and started toward the tree. A club wouldn't hurt the bear any but it might make her leave Little Jim, and I decided I'd give my life for him if I had to. In my mind I could see him being ripped all to pieces; and if ever I prayed in my life, I did right then.

Little Jim's face was terrible to look at, but he held onto the gun. Then he shoved the barrel forward to protect himself from getting knocked down, kind of like he was using it for a sword. And when the bear lunged, the muzzle of the gun ran right into her mouth and down into her throat.

Just that moment Big Jim and all of us screamed, *"Shoot! Shoot!"*

*And Little Jim shot!*

\* \* \*

I can hear the bear roaring every time I think of it; and I can see her thrashing around with the gun barrel stuck in her throat, and all the time, she was dying. It's awful to see a bear die,

116

and I don't like to think about it; but it was a lot easier to see her die than it would have been to see Little Jim or any of the rest of the Sugar Creek Gang or Tom Till.

I ran home as quick as I could after the bear died to get my dad and a camera. Afterward when some men came and skinned the bear, they found the bullet had gone right into the bear's neck and broken it.

With everybody helping, we caught the little brown-nosed cub, and Little Jim got him for a pet like he had wanted to in the first place.

When little Tom Till came down out of that tree alive he was shaking like a leaf. And do you know? When you looked at him up real close he had the prettiest blue eyes, even if they were filled with tears and his face was dirty where his dirty fists had tried to wipe the tears away. He didn't look like a mean boy at all anymore. Anyway, none of us boys hated him after that.

On the way home, Little Jim wanted to carry the rifle, and we let him do it 'cause he was the hero. As soon as the newspapers of the country found out about it, they sent reporters. Little

Jim's picture and the bear's went all over the country. It made us feel good and mighty proud to have him belong to our gang.

Anyway, that's the end of this story. Nothing of any special importance happened until school started that fall. Maybe I'd better tell you that Circus' dad never took another drop of whiskey or beer as long as he lived; and his mother got well and it was a happy family from then on, which goes to show what Jesus can do for a boy's dad.

I still kind of hate to stop writing though, 'cause I'd like you to know about Old Man Paddler and what happened one day that winter. It was on Saturday, I think, and the gang got to wondering if the old man had enough firewood to keep him warm. It had been a long time since we were up there, so we decided to take some groceries and things and go to see him. There were high drifts everywhere and it was as cold as Santa Claus' nose, but not too cold for boys to be out if they were dressed warm enough.

But that's another story, which I hope I won't forget to write for you some time soon. I'm not nearly as forgetful as I used to be before our old red rooster died. Say, it was the funniest thing, the way Dad killed him, not at all like the way I killed our Thanksgiving turkey that fall.

Moody Press, a ministry of the Moody Bible Institute, is designed for education, evangelization and edification. If we may assist you in knowing more about Christ and the Christian life, please write us without obligation to: Moody Press, c/o MLM, Chicago, Illinois 60610.